THE DEMONS OF GOTHAM

THE DEMONS OF GOTHAM

TIM O'LEARY

Copyright © 2023 Tim O'leary.

All rights reserved. No part of this book may be reproduced, stored, or transmitted by any means—whether auditory, graphic, mechanical, or electronic—without written permission of both publisher and author, except in the case of brief excerpts used in critical articles and reviews. Unauthorized reproduction of any part of this work is illegal and is punishable by law.

ISBN: 979-8-89031-549-6 (sc)
ISBN: 979-8-89031-550-2 (hc)
ISBN: 979-8-89031-551-9 (e)

Because of the dynamic nature of the Internet, any web addresses or links contained in this book may have changed since publication and may no longer be valid. The views expressed in this work are solely those of the author and do not necessarily reflect the views of the publisher, and the publisher hereby disclaims any responsibility for them.

One Galleria Blvd., Suite 1900, Metairie, LA 70001
(504) 702-6708
1-888-421-2397

For those who are righteous and believe in the Liberties as established in the United States Constitution, let everyone thrive and sustain himself in the God-given right to freedom and ability to choose.

OTHER SHAWN CRAWFORD ADVENTURES BY TIM O'LEARY

The Gateway

Time Dimensions

The Dimensional Gateway

The Assigner

Missions

Nathan

Christopher

The Narragansett Trail: A Horror Story

Emily: A Horror Story

The Cradle of evil: A Horror Story

Tim O'Hara: The Early Years

The O'Hara Brothers: The Prof Years

LT. Tim O'Hara, United States Navy

Sancha

Warriors

Knights

OTHER SHAWN CRAWFORD ADVENTURES BY TIM O'LEARY

Nowhere To Run: A Story of Maternal Abuse

The Ethereal Presence: A Time Travel Adventure Joey

Kennebunk: A Horror Story

The Last War

Aruba

The Portal

The Entity

The Entity's Child

The Entity's Chosen

CDR J. Hunter King

Saving Kuwait: A Soldier's Memoir

A Demon Tetralogy

The Entity's War

The Extinction of Planet Kepler

Shawn Crawford: The Later Years

Tim O'Hara: A Tale of Two Lives

CONTENTS

Characters xi
Prologue xxi

Gotham, Maine 1
The Pandemic 7
Sydney, 2078 to Gotham, 2024 11
F-93b Leopard Advanced Fighter 15
Illness Reaction 27
The First One Hundred Days 39

Chaotic Days 47

One Year Later In Maine.. 51

The Gubernatorial Term of Office 59

Rising Political Star.. 69

Soaring Political Advances.. 89

Demonic Retaliation 95

Days of Danger 103

Final Vote and Justice... 111

Author Bibliography 115

CHARACTERS

FIRST LIEUTENANT WILL CARUSO: Royal Australian Plane Captain to the F-42A Tiger Shark and B-193B Advanced Fighter Aircraft. Highly intelligent, irreverent and carefree spirit and Crew Chief with a meticulous eye problem-solving regarding all Fixed-Wing and Rotary-Wing Aircraft in the Defense inventory. Awarded the Meritorious Service Medal for his accomplishments in aircraft fighter support to the Royal Australian Air Force. Member of The Entity's Inner Circle. Time era origination: 2074.

STAFF SERGEANT MADELYN COFFILL: Royal Australian Air Force, Chief Administrative Assistant 'Gatekeeper' for Marshal Allison Morrison. Very efficient in the performance of her duties while displaying an intemperate exterior but harboring a heart of gold and boundless inner kindness. Chief Guardian to Colette Roberts-Crawford in the absence of Lady Christine Roberts. Time era origination: 2074.

SIR STEVEN SHAWN CRAWFORD: Air Marshal, Royal Australian Air Force, former Lieutenant Colonel, United States Army, Husband to Lady Christine Roberts, Father to Christopher and Colette, Pilot, OH-58D Kiowa Warrior, AH-1G Cobra Gunship and RAH-66 Comanche Attack Helicopters. The F-42A Tiger Shark and F-193B Leopard Advanced Stealth Fighter Aircraft. Moral, modest, and irreverent contributor to every major of personnel involvement. Chief expert in the understanding of Gateway/Wormhole events. Principal deterrent to the assassination attempts on the lives of various historical figures. Audacious and fierce devotee toward protecting the rights of those oppressed. Twice awarded the United States Medal of Honor, a Hero in the Third World War, Seventh Degree Black Belt Martial Arts Specialist and Expert in the art of Silent Killing. Speaks eight foreign languages and former Delta Force Black Ops Member. Triple Ace against enemy Air Force Aggressors in aerial combat. Holds a Doctorate Degree in Advanced Aeronautical Engineering and Quantum Mechanics with Degrees in Economics and Chemistry from Georgia Southern University. Member of the Australian Government's Intelligence Agency. Never misses a good Beef Wellington dinner. Favorite of The Entity. Time era origination: 2017.

CHRISTINE ROBERTS-CRAWFORD: The temporal Mother of Christopher and Colette Roberts-Crawford. Wife of Shawn Crawford. F-22 Raptor Pilot who recorded more than 15 aerial 'kills' while flying against German Nazi Aircraft during a time travel sojourn. Given the Title of 'Lady' Christine for her role in saving the Australian Ambassador in the year 2074. Proficient in flying both the F-42A Tiger Shark as well as the F-193B Leopard Advanced Stealth Fighter Aircraft. An Agent of The Entity. Time era origination: 2017.

CHRISTOPHER ROBERTS-CRAWFORD: The temporal Son of Shawn and Christine. Seventh Degree Black Belt Martial Arts Specialist. Speaks eight foreign languages. An advanced Fighter Pilot with more than 10 aerial 'kills' making him a Double Ace. Speaks at World Symposiums relating to his knowledge of time travel, quantum physics and the Universe. Is 16 years of age. An Agent and Son of The Entity. Time era origination: Always.

COLETTE ROBERTS-CRAWFORD: The temporal Daughter of Shawn and Christine. Loves to tweak her Father's nose when the latter is mischievous. Has the power to bring individuals back from the dead. An Advanced Fighter Pilot at the age of 10 years old. Precocious, loving and caring for those in need. An Agent and Daughter of The Entity. Time era origination: Always.

JOLIE O'LEARY-CRAWFORD: Cousin to Sir Shawn Crawford through her marriage to Thomas Crawford. Heir to a billion-dollar inheritance following the sudden death of her Husband Thomas. Time era origination: 2017.

EMILY: A perpetual 12-year old Girl who having ability to conquer Evil by the use of a Medallion with an ancient script. Defeated the Demon along the Narragansett Trail in Gotham, Maine with Sir Shawn Crawford and Tim O'Leary. Overcame another Demon during the Third Crusades. An Agent of The Entity. Time era origination: Always.

NATHAN DOERFLER: Physician's Assistant who was brought back to life several times by The Entity. Seventh Degree Black Belt in the Martial Arts. An Agent of The Entity who has traveled through time on numerous occasions to fulfill missions give to him by The Entity. Holds two Doctoral Degrees from Georgia Southern University in Medical Science and Physics. Cousin to Sir Shawn Crawford. Stopped the assassination of President John F. Kennedy in Dallas, Texas in November 1963. Time era origination: 2017.

ROBERTO "BOB" GONZALES: Air Commodore for Rotary-Wing Operations Aviation Helicopter Group, amicably referred to as 'The Chief'. Unit Historian and renowned Helicopter Pilot commanding respect for his exception helicopter flying skills. Awarded the Distinguished Service Cross and Silver Star for aerial performance of duty beyond all expectations against opposing enemy forces. Principal Paternal Influence and Mentor to the totally irreverent Shawn Crawford. Back-seat Radar Intercept Officer in the F-22B Raptor during anti-drug related missions in South America. Presently serves the Australian Sydney Air Defense Force as the Air Commodore, Pilot of the F-42A Tiger Shark Stealth Fighter, RAH-66 Comanche and

AH-1GCobra Attack Helicopters. Chief Rotary-Wing Instructor for the Australian Sydney Air Defense Force.

ADMIRAL J. HUNTER KING: Charismatic Special Operations [SEAL/Delta Force] Leader fluent in seven languages specializing in Arabic and Swahili. Seventh Degree Black Belt in the Art of Silent Killing. Holds a dual Doctorate Degree from American University in International Studies and from the Massachusetts Institute of Technology (M.I.T.) in Advanced Fusion Quantum Mechanics. Built his first mini-jet fighter at the age of 11. Married to equally charismatic Kathleen. Veteran of the African Wars. Time era origination: 2017.

DONALD LAGACE: CIA Operative and Time Traveler, Agent for The Entity, Principal Organizer in the operation causing abrupt cessation of the Third World War hostilities in 2018. Part-time Musician and Contributor to famous Scores such as The Star-Spangled Banner. Time era origination: Always.

MARSHAL ALLISON MORRISON: Senior Officer commanding the Australian Sydney Air Defense Base. Wife of Air Chief Marshal Michael O'Leary. Outstanding and charismatic Leader of all aerial forces on the Continent of Australia. Directed victory against the incursion of African Federation Forces into Australia. Time era origination: 2074.

AIR CHIEF MARSHAL MICHAEL O'LEARY: Royal Australian Air Force, former Lieutenant Colonel, United States Air Force, Husband to Marshal Allison Marshall. F-42A Tiger Shark Stealth Fighter Pilot and Mentor to Sir Shawn Crawford. Gained Fighter Pilot Ace status when he traveled back in time to conduct aerial battles against aggressors during World War II and the Korean War. Wounded in action. Time era origination: 2053.

SANCHA: The Automated Voice Recognition System aboard the newest Attack Stealth Fighter Aircraft, the F-98A Stingray. Responds only to voice recognition commands given by Sir Shawn Crawford.

GRACE: The Red Cross Worker who was sought after to work for the Central Intelligence Agency following the 7.9 Iranian earthquake. Doubles as an Employee for the Homa Hotel in Bandar Abbas, Iran. Serves as a key figure in the success of Lt. Timothy O'Hara's mission to eliminate a notorious Iranian terrorist.

JOLIE; Entity Agent assisting Lt. Timothy O'Hara in the assassination of an Iranian General Officer in Bandar Abbas, Iran. Niece to elderly Franz who ferries individual across the Strait of Hormuz to the Iranian mainland.

FRANZ: A captain of a 20-foot fishing boat that doubles as a transportation asset for The Entity in time of need. Uncle to Jolie. Enables a Protection Detail of two massive hounds named Mickey and Minnie.

KYLE: Versatile Agent of The Entity. Friend to Jolie and Franz. Great sense of humor and resourceful when a mission is on the line

THE ENTITY: An Intergalactic Being who is the Champion of Good over Evil. Employs Agents to traverse through a Gateway that enables them to go back into the past and deny assassination attempts on lives of influential individuals who serve only what is Good and Righteous in their own time eras. Utilizes Sir Shawn Crawford as His Agent to correct world injustices. Time era origination: Always.

PROLOGUE

If one were to look upward at the right moment, you would have seen bright dots of light, six of them, falling slowly out of the sky. Their separation was exact with two leading the others, then two side by side and final two mirroring the second group. The second two then split, one each falling with the lead lights on either side. The third group did the same and became the end objects creating a falling line of light to the earth.

The grouping passed through a thin cloud layer causing the vapor to spark violently. The lights increased in size the closer they got to the ground. When they were three feet above the surface, they didn't quite stop their descent, but floated gently the remaining distance until they touched down. A loud rumbling sound, like a thunderclap, echoed through the area, almost as if their presence was being announced dramatically and emphatically. It was two o'clock in the morning.

The lights began to take humanoid shape and continued to change until six individual beings stood without moving. There were six men altogether. Their features continued to develop until the light surrounding them ceased to exist. They stood silent for a moment before the Leader motioned for them to spread out. They were at the edge of a clearing and each figure started floating as one into the tree line. Their eyes gleamed a solid red to conflict with a complexion that was alabaster white. They stopped suddenly and kept very still. One of the forms floated ahead and stopped behind a thick strand of bush that fanned out at least three feet from its center.

In a small clearing was a group of teens hovering over a camp fire. A radio was playing softly nearby. One of the individuals passed a pipe to another who, in turn, did the same until all six individuals had received its contents. They were talking about nothing in particular, subjects that flood forth when individuals were 'high' on some narcotic.

The five other beings joined the one who had gone forward. The Leader looked at the others and sent a telepathic message to the others. As one, they came out of hiding and fell on the group of teenagers who screamed in fear. As one of them tried to run away from the clearing, he was cut down by an electrical charge emitted from the hand of one of the beings. The torso of the individual was struck in the center of the back causing the teen to lurch forward. The charge exited his body in the front and he fell lifeless to the ground. The other 5 at the camp fire fared no better. Two were decapitated by the electrical charge thrown by a Demon and the remaining three were completely incinerated.

The radio continued to play its soft music as the camp fire began to lessen in intensity. The Demons formed a circle around what remained of the dead teens and joined hands. The ashes of the youth rose and were directed into the fire by the Leader. Voices of the dead screamed as their souls were consumed by the dying flames.

This Town was ripe for devastation and extreme turmoil. The Leader of the Demons smiled to the others and indicated that this was where they were going to establish a fear so great that its citizens would want to leave and never come back. They unclasped their hands and together, as one, they floated from the clearing and onto New Poland Road. They reached the cemetery and chose certain tomb stones to reside in during the course of the day. Little did the Gotham residents realize that their Town had been invaded and infected with terror.

GOTHAM, MAINE

Established in 1736, the Town of Gotham, Maine served as a bedroom community for those traveling to work in nearby Poland each day. Its size was expansive and separated into sub-sections, such as Small Falls and Black Rock communities. Gotham didn't have a Mayor but relied on its Town Council to direct its affairs for the Town. All in all, there were seven members on the Board who met once a month as an ancillary duty to their normal and daily employment elsewhere.

The Council was a group of individuals who played 'politics' with their elected power, and decided issues on the merit of each in terms of need to benefit the wealthy. Of course, there were always dissenters who felt that their concerns were summarily excused as being not important. For the most part, the Town taxes were expended to suit the critical needs first in terms of sorely needed renovations and other ancillary measures to benefit the Town, or, more precisely, the Town's elite. It was not unusual for the Town to approve a specific area of work for the wealthy neighborhoods while the poorer sections of Gotham continued to suffer and deteriorate. There was talk of kickbacks to some of the Council membership.

There were a few individuals who thought the revenue should be spent more on entertainment, such as a movie theater, a McDonald's and even a large shopping center. Residents had to drive the miles to go into South Poland and the Mall to find what they wanted or needed. With the land available to build, failure to do so rankled many members of the community. Side walks along Route 250, or Main Street, were a walking hazard. The local cemeteries were uncared for as the majority of graves were grown over with weed and high grass. And, then, there was the traffic by-pass problem for commuters traveling from West to East and return on a daily basis. For the past 50 years, a thoroughfare around the Town was promised, but never completed, let alone initiated. Traffic backed up from the center of Town at least two miles during the period 3:30 through 6:30 pm daily on Route 250 leading from neighboring Southbrook. There was a lot of frustration on the part of some that when the issue was elevated, it was dismissed as non-important. Of course, those doing the dismissing didn't have to endure the long traffic lights and vehicles negotiating through the Town.

This latter issue reached a boiling point during the Summer of 2022 when motorists appeared to lose all patience with the lack of initiative on the part of the Council. Individuals would become angry with another motorist in front of them if the latter was courteous enough to let a vehicle from a side street enter the line of traffic. People began getting out of their trucks and cars and walking up to the motorist in front of them and berating their good will. There were even instances of arguments turning physical on occasion. As the Summer season wore on, the situation was exacerbated with maintenance crews performing road work during the height of the rush hour. It eventually got out of control.

One individual got so angry and frustrated that he pulled out his semi-automatic pistol, walked up to the vehicle in front of him and shot the driver in the head. The local police had been defunded and their numbers patrolling the Town were at an absolute minimum. There was no safety relief valve to stop aggravated situations from occurring. Very soon, there was anarchy in the Town of Gotham. People of the Town demanded answers to all of the thorny problems plaguing them. Even the smallest of issues was elevated to a high priority whether it made sense of not. Of course, the Town Council couldn't and sometimes wouldn't take these arguments under advisement and began 'putting its head in the sand' in the hope that they would go away with time and disinterest.

One evening, a Town Councilor's home was firebombed in the middle of the night. Fortunately, no one was seriously injured, although the entire home was destroyed by fire. Those without means, compared to the elite, were greatly discouraged about how their lives were being manipulated.

They were doing something about it. Many on their side felt that burning down a home and putting its residents in a deadly situation was too extreme.

But, as time moved along, the poor in Town decided to congregate in front of the Town Hall when the monthly meeting was being held. As one could attend the meeting and contribute by asking questions about the status of one issue or another, the meeting was totally packed by citizens who demanded answers. When the attendees were not satisfied with the response to their concerns, they became boisterous to the extent that the meeting had to be halted. The Council members left the building only to find a mob waiting for them outside. As the members retreated to their vehicles, some of the dissenters began punching two of the Councilors who were pushed to the pavement. They were beaten severely before law enforcement arrived on the scene. No one was arrested as a medical vehicle took the two officials to the local hospital.

The six Demons watched the entire confrontation with great interest. The Leader telepathically told the others that the Town of Gotham was ripe for total insurrection. A little more pressure applied to the psychological effect of not having demands met appeared appropriate. The officials were doing their work for them which was to sow discontent between the rich and the poor through a socialistic vision of governing. Gotham, Maine was on the cusp of total rebellion.

THE PANDEMIC

The Town Council elections were held the following month. During the interim time when the home was fire bombed and election day, the citizens of Gotham became aware that six newcomers in Town had decided to run for seats on the Council. One worked at Gotham Savings Bank, another at the local hardware store, the Manager at Burger King and the others were self-employed in the service industry all vying for a seat. The odd thing about these individuals was that each individual was not considered an attention getter, but simply a nice person. That perception changed after the Councilor's house burned to the ground.

The day following the destruction of the home by fire, each of the six candidates experienced an event in their homes at the same time, 9:00 pm. As each person rested or performed a menial task within the home, a beam of light descended upon their house and completely consumed the structure. The home gleamed brightly then stopped. No one in the area noticed the anomaly. It appeared to be a natural act by nature as a thunderstorm was moving through the area and lightning was hitting everywhere. It was anything but a natural event as the residents of these homes were to find out, however.

Each beam of light represented one of the Demon figures. It infused itself into the Town Council Candidate causing each individual to become nauseous. Simultaneously, the men decided to take the same over the counter medication for an upset stomach. Relieving the discomfort somewhat, the individuals began sneezing and coughing consistently.

Each developed a fever of over 101-degrees. As one, they went to bed and slept fitfully through the night.

They all awakened felling fine and though the previous evening's discomfort was no longer evident in their physical systems, the infection instilled the evening before now lay dormant in their bodies. Each person left his home and reported in to work. They greeted the same individuals by shaking hands or by wishing the other person a 'good morning' as they passed by. Tiny modules of water were emitted when the greeting was given. These entered the other person's nasal tract and continued throughout the body. Four hours later, the recipient of these modules began to feel uncomfortable. Each remained at work and continued to relate to others, clients and/or customers, who also were infected through casual or professional conversation. The beginning of a pandemic had just occurred and its effects on the Town would become devastating.

SYDNEY, 2078 TO GOTHAM, 2024

Sir Shawn Crawford and his good Friend Admiral J. Hunter King were cruising at 8,000 feet above Northwestern Australia in a sleek-looking advanced fighter aircraft known as the F-93B Leopard. King was at the controls and sitting in the right seat, or First Officer's chair. Crawford just finished eating a sandwich when a strange radio transmission came through over their UHF communications system. It was a string of numbers repeated over and over again. They were given in two sections of eight digits each followed by a single set of 2020.

Shawn turned the volume up slightly and behind the numbers given was a static message as though someone was calling for help in a far away location. Crawford began writing down the numbers as King continued flying the aircraft.

"What do you make of that transmission, Coach?" he asked Shawn.

"If I'm not mistaken, Kemo Sabe, these appear to be Earth coordinates. And the '2024' at the end represents the year at that location. Let me pull out my map and see if any of this makes sense."

After a moment's study, he turned to Hunter and said that if these were indeed coordinates, they correlated with a location on the map called Gotham, Maine. This was a place that Shawn was altogether too familiar with.

Years before, Crawford had battled a group of Demons at an old Friend's home. Tim and Lynn O'Leary lived on Main Street in the Town that had been infiltrated by shape-shifting demons. Crawford, O'Leary and a Doctor Wesolowski had eliminated the threat through the help of The Entity, an Intergalactic Being who represented Good in the battle against Evil in the Cosmos. These beings attempted to take over the Town and finally destroy it and its inhabitants for injustices committed against Native Americans during the 17th Century.

"Coach," Shawn began, "Looks like an overall request for help from some old friends in Maine, the United States. Can't imagine these coordinates came from them though. I bet our Blueness, The Entity, has a heavy hand in all of this"

Off on the distance, one single cloud appeared at their twelve o'clock position. It had a familiar bluish tint to it. Hunter looked at Shawn who grinned and said, "Hang on, Coach. Looks like we're going to be late for dinner at the Club this evening."

They entered the cloud and the Leopard shook violently for about 15 seconds. When they exited, they found themselves over a large lake. On the shoreline completely around the body of water were smattering of snow deposits from a recent late

Fall storm. Then a controller broadcast On Guard Frequency the following:

"Unidentified aircraft over Sebago Lake, this is Poland Tower. Please state your intentions."

"Poland Tower, we are a Leopard F-93B Advanced Fighter Aircraft, squawking 1200, at 8,000 feet. Request permission to land at Poland."

"Leopard 93B, squawk 4701 and ident."

Hunter punched in the code and hit the ident button. "Leopard 93B, you are 15 miles Northwest of the Poland Airport. Winds are negligible. Report entering downwind for Runway 28," replied the Controller. Hunter repeated the instructions and turned to Shawn and said, "Old home week reunion, Coach?"

"Have no idea, Coach. But, if The Entity sent us here, it had to be for a very good reason. I hope my Friends are alright. Maybe Lynn has some of her homemade chili on the stove."

"That would be great. But, Shawn, if memory serves this is the era when the Great Pandemic hit the world. It caused the death of over a half million U.S.

F-93B LEOPARD ADVANCED FIGHTER

Citizens and three million totally on the Planet. I read a little further about the years 2020 – 2024 and this is also when the State went from a Liberal Control Party to one of Socialism. We'll be in the early stages of that developing today. I also noted that the newly-elected Town Councilor here is a staunch Socialist who is looking to turn the State of Maine upside down at some point in the future. This should turn out to be an interesting visit."

"I guess we'll be wearing a mask in public. Really don't have anything like that on me. Do you?"

Hunter then noticed a couple of face masks hanging on the far side of their seats. "Where did these come from? Or, should I even ask the question?"

They made their approach to the Poland-Southbrook International Airport and parked the Leopard on the General Aviation Ramp. The fuel truck came over stopped about half way and the driver just gawked at the futuristic jet. Shawn climbed down the ladder and approached the vehicle.

"Yes, I know. I get that look all the time. Just fill it up with JP-5. It might take a lot fuel, just so that you know."

Crawford had to show the driver where the fuel intake was for the poor man was so confused and bewildered at the sight of the aircraft in front of him.

"Be gentle with the girl, Sir. She can get ornery when not treated with kindness and a caring attitude."

Hunter joined Shawn and they walked into the Fixed Based Operations (FBO) Building. They donned their masks as they entered, went through the length of the building and out the back door. There, waiting for them with a big smile on their faces were Tim and Lynn O'Leary. They greeted one another warmly and jumped into Lynn's Honda CRV. They left the airport area and proceeded through a portion of Poland to Gotham on Route 250. They arrived 25 minutes after the Leopard touchdown in Poland. "So, Timmy, what's going on here in little Sleepy Hollow?"

"Politics are what's going on here in Gotham. The Town is run by a Council with one agenda in mind and that is Socialism. Gotham has turned into a slum Town with no regard for the decency and privacy of the common person from the Middle Class. The taxes for the purchase of basic commodities are outrageous. Town Government is using the pandemic as leverage to gain more and more public funding from Washington. Churches are being shut down and secondary school education is at a standstill victimized by virtual learning. The kids are suffering from lack of peer group dynamics. It's a real mess.

"There is another matter I wanted to talk to you about. I believe that we are being influenced by beings, not humans, who wish to see our capitalistic way of life eliminated for the more State run Government socialistic views. I was finishing a jog one early morning and my track took me through a clearing in the woods.

"As I went into the open area, a radio was playing music and a camp fire had been reduced to embers. I slowed down a bit to see if anyone was around, but saw no one. I did notice mounds of ash spread out here and there within the clearing and thought it strange. When I saw bone fragments within the ash, I knew that a sacrificial ritual had been conducted. I stopped jogging for a moment and stood there listening to the radio music and beginning to get a bad feeling about this place. It felt unholy and my skin started to crawl. A dog began to bark on the other side of the wood line moments later. I decided to leave right away and started jogging until I reached my house five minutes later.

"There is something going on here in this Town and it's not good. Reports of physical altercations are being mentioned daily. People are beginning to react negatively over the smallest issue resulting in innocent people getting traumatized."

Shawn looked at Hunter and they both knew why they were in Gotham, Maine. The Entity does not send His emissaries on missions of no consequence. There was definitely an Evil force working its way into the lives of Gotham people. The Town's administration never behaved in a manner so negatively that contradicted the well-being of its citizens.

There was a loud clap that sounded like thunder at that moment and all turned around and looked toward the back sliding door. A circular black cloud had materialized and was hovering some one hundred feet above the O'Leary's pool. From it, six beams of light descended onto the pavement nearby.

When they touched the surface, the beams took human form and stood facing the house, Hunter turned to Tim and asked, "Friends of yours, Coach?"

Before anyone could say anything, one of the humanoid forms pointed its arm toward the house and a laser of white energy shot forward toward the home. Shawn yelled for everyone to get down as the streak of electricity hit the house. The entire back wall was obliterated with a huge 'bang'. Shawn and the others had hit the floor and one by one they slowly recovered to their feet. King looked outside and saw that their 'uninvited guests' were still standing motionless outside. Then all received a telepathic message from one of the Demons.

"Return to your time, Shawn Crawford. We do not want you here. This is your final warning. If we find that you are meddling in our affairs, you will pay dearly with your souls."

The figures mutated quickly into light beams and rose into the air until they were no longer seen. At that moment, a pack of huge wolves came out of the clearing behind the house. There were six of them. One by one, they ambled up to where the Demons had shown themselves and sat down in a row by the pool. Their eyes were the lightest blue color in the spectrum. One of the massive beasts stepped forward slowly and placed its huge body prone on the ground. When this one was settled on the pavement, the others copied the first until all six were laying down with their heads facing Shawn and the others on the deck.

The lead wolf then sat up and telepathically told them that they were sent by The Entity to protect and defend against the injustices being committed by the citizens of Gotham. They were the stopgap from increasing violence and react to wrongdoing by first remaining in the shadows and then taking action when there was critical need to do so. They would be unobtrusive. By this, they demonstrated its meaning.

One by one, each shape-shifted into a human being, Three men and women stood before them. Their appearance would be recognized as everyday people who did their business when out and about in Town. At night, they would patrol the streets separately and quell any problems that developed by those seeking to take advantage of the weak and elderly. And they would do so as wolves lurking nearby when a need arose.

Tim turned around and looked at his home. The room off of the deck was a shambles. Fortunately, there was no fire to put out. And, for some unknown reason, the explosion did not draw the attention of the local police. It was clear that the Demons wanted to send a message that not only got their attention, but caused much for consideration.

Crawford walked into what was left of the living room and stood there for a long moment. Hunter and Tim joined him. Before anyone could speak, a bluish cloud had appeared about a thousand feet in the air above the damaged home. From it, two futuristic aircraft shot out and banked ninety degrees toward them. One by one, they landed in trail.

As their engines spooled down, both pilots exited his aircraft and walked over to Shawn and the others. Crawford raised an eyebrow when he saw who these two pilots were. He wasn't exactly happy to see both of them.

"Christopher and Colette, what are you doing here?

"Father, since you had not returned to Base when you were supposed to, we decided to take a training flight. We were cleared by Michael O'Leary to launch. I do believe the Deputy Commander felt that you were in need of reinforcements. And since, The Entity allowed us entry through the Dimensional Gateway, we knew that coming here was the right thing to do."

"Your Mother is not going to be happy when she learns that you've gone Dimensional Gateway hopping. Now that you both are here, you remember the O'Leary's, don't you?"

They all greeted one another, Colette gave a big hug to Lynn and Tim while Christopher shook their hands. Hunter acknowledged them both. Christopher then asked that everyone step onto the lawn area beyond the pool fence. As all did so, he remained by the deck just outside the destroyed living room. Christopher raised his right arm and pointed toward the destruction. With his left arm, he made a circular motion and a bluish cloud whirled before him. The home was completely enveloped by the vapor and remained that way for 30 seconds.

When Christopher lowered his arms to his side, the bluish cloud began to dissipate rapidly. In seconds, the others saw the Boy standing before a completely renovated living room. It looked like nothing had happened to it.

Christopher went over to the others on the lawn and told Tim and Lynn that they wouldn't have to worry about window leaks any longer. And, he looked at Tim and said that there was a new Sony 75-inch Smart HD TV sitting on a brand new stand in the corner of the room, courtesy of The Entity.

"Mrs. O'Leary, you can now watch Judge Judy in an innovative vibrant color that has yet to be marketed in Maine. Congratulations on being the first Consumer to acquire this soon-to-be sought after item.

Lynn and Tim thanked Christopher as they walked over to the back deck door. The others followed them through the sliding glass doorway and sat down on brand new stylistic furniture, Lynn stared at her new room in amazement. She couldn't thank Christopher enough who replied that The Entity takes care of His own. There was a resounding chuckle coming from the wood line area that was heard by all.

"Tim and Lynn, you two individuals have been supportive of the Crawford Family for years now. It is My time to show appreciation for everything you have done in support of the missions given to Shawn and his friends. Please enjoy your new addition to your home."

Shawn said, "Your Vastness, You are truly a Prince among Princes. Now, about that addition to our home in 2078, could I have it painted in lavender?"

There was a hearty laugh in response that died out into nothing. Shawn merely smiled and shrugged his shoulders at his two children. Colette tweaked her Father's nose.

The wolves that had turned into humans had all, but one, vanished from the property. He had morphed back into the wolf shape and laid down by the pool on the pavement. Its blue eyes rested on the inhabitants of the O'Leary home as it stood guard against any evil that might befall Tim and Lynn.

Illness Reaction

The day following the teen massacre at the camp fire, parents of each individual failing to shop at his/her home called local law enforcement and reported a missing person. Meanwhile, a couple of boys were at the baseball field adjacent to the wooded area encompassing the clearing where the teens were murdered. A ball was hit into the woods and one of the boy's dogs chased after it into the brush. When the dog did not immediately return, one of the boys decided to go look for him. He called for the dog as he cleared a path into the woods. He froze when he began to hear soft music coming from an area just ahead of him. When he entered the clearing, the dog was lying down beside several mound of ashes. The smell was repugnant.

Beside the ashes were tangible items that couldn't have been consumed in fire, such as three rings, necklaces and coin money. The youth panicked and called for his dog to come with him out of the clearing and back to the ball field. When he cleared the wood line, he trotted over to his friend and told him what he had seen. The second boy was a little older and decided to call the police rather than to do some further investigating.

The local authorities arrived and began their forensic activity. The hardware found was put into a plastic bag. Samples of the ash were taken and preserved for submission to the lab for analysis. The boys were questioned and the affected area was roped off until laboratory personnel could identify what the ashes represented. Parents of the missing children feared the worst.

The following morning, the teenagers from the camp fire all returned home. Each individual was happy to be there and could not tell exactly what happened that night at the fire. They all appeared normal with one exception. There were no typical mood swings that this age group normally exhibited. On the other hand, each individual appeared overly optimistic about everything going on in the world. The parents were pleased about the turn-about attitude toward school and other events in their children's lives for the immediate future. Then, when circumstances dictated a response that would be typical of previous behavior relating to frustration, anger or some other form of non-acceptance, nothing happened in this manner. Intuitively, mothers began to take a closer look at how their children reacted to situations affecting them daily. They became concerned that their children were not acting according to the expectations of the parent given the issue at hand. Fathers were informed about the change and attempted to talk to their children in round about terms about their feelings and whether anything bothered them. Each child responded that they couldn't be happier and life was simply great. Each parent's alert system kicked in and they decided to monitor the actions of their children more closely without being obtrusive, until both the fathers and mothers in each family began to feel ill. Then the concern switched dramatically to the well-being of the parents. One by one, the teenagers' parents succumbed to an illness that doctors could not diagnose. As the second parent passed on from the mysterious malady, the teen in that family simply disappeared from the Gotham community. There was no indication that he had left to be with a relative. Nor was there a note explaining the disappearance. He were just gone!

At a remote place in rural Maine, the camp fire teenagers all met. They were now orphans as all parents had succumbed to the same illness. As with the first, these children left no message about where they were going. They vanished from sight.

It was ten o'clock in the evening. Each teen was directed to this location by some inner voice that translated dialogue into coordinates. They arrived via hitch hiking on back roads, a journey that took several days to complete. As the last one entered the cabin, one of the teens assumed the role of leadership. The five others began asking why they were sent to this place. The Leader answered that it was a mystery to him as well, but believed all would be made clear very soon. One of the boys said that he hoped so because he was more than a little hungry. Two others echoed the same feeling.

One of them looked out the cabin window and saw six beams of light falling from the sky. It appeared that they were going to drop in the vicinity of their building. He pointed them out to the others and they turned to watch the lights descend in front of their cabin. They sparked once and morphed into six humanoids that were familiar to them all. Two got up and started to run from the cabin, but they were stopped in place once they had gone out the door. The other four stood transfixed and feeling that they were going to go through another episode of the camp fire experience. Then, one voice from the humanoid group spoke to them telepathically.

"Do not be afraid. We are here to help and guide you on your journey of immense importance to this Country. Please, all sit down in the cabin and we will explain what is happening to you. Do not fear; we did not return to you to harm you.

"You may refer to us as The High Authority. And you six will be the instruments of our agenda to take over the world. Caleb shall be your Leader and will guide you through the process of events that we want all of you to participate in for the purpose of attaining socialistic goals for this Country. We have just shared our vision with him and he, in turn, will present it to you. Each of you will play a significant role in completing our agenda. It is vitally important that you follow the orders given to you exactly as given. There is no other option for you. Should you fail to comply with all directives, your soul this time will be lost forever."

Before them, a piece of white parchment paper appeared on the table. One of the boys nodded to himself as if he were expecting this to appear. He turned to the six beings and bowed before them.

Each of the six figures then turned into a bright light for a brief moment and disappeared. The boys looked at one another with total fear showing. They were too stunned to speak. Finally, one of them got up and went to the door and closed it. He looked around the room to the others and introduced himself as Caleb.

The Leader of the group, a teen a year older than the others, stood at the head of a table and looked down at the other individuals. They were now on their own for good and had the ability to create their own future. Now was the beginning to take over not only the State of Maine, but the entire country.

The Leader unrolled a parchment paper and placed it in the middle of the table. On it were the key

United States Government positions listed beginning with the President of the United States. The others shown were the Vice-President, the Secretary of State, the Secretary of Defense, Treasury Secretary and Secretary of Health and Human Services. The Leader took out a marker and placed the name of a teen sitting before him against one of the positions outlined on the paper.

"In two years, no one will recognize you. As a matter of fact, you will not recognize yourselves. Our bodies have transcended the normal growth process and you no longer are 15 or 16 years old. You will age exponentially gaining ten years in age every succeeding twelve months. During this time, you will avail yourself to learning everything you can about the position that has your name marked beside it. I mean everything.

"We have all murdered our parents with the disease that we are able to spread by mere contact with another. As you become familiar with the title of your intended United States position, you will have the power to eliminate anyone who seeks to stop you from achieving your goal. We belong now to the demonic group that made us who we are today. They are our Masters and we report to them, and only them. Each Demon has been assigned to one of us as a Mentor to insure that we accomplish our end game of taking over this Country. Failure is not an option. Your very lives depend on your commitment to reaching your goal of attaining your Government position. Do you have any questions, or concerns. There should be none of the latter."

Back in Gotham, citizens went about their daily lives, spreading the virus. Exponentially, the disease had been given to each person the Candidate for the Town Council had met. These people, in turn, passed it along to their families and to those with whom they worked daily. Within two weeks, the Poland Hospitals were being overwhelmed with new patients, not only from Gotham, but from neighboring Towns where friends and relatives of the Gothamites lived. Medical care givers were suffering in great numbers also. The

Center for Disease Control was asked to step in and evaluate the new strain of flu, or so they thought it might be. When patients began dying by the 10's each day, and not from underlying conditions, the medical professionals were at a loss in terms of how to treat it. Normal medications for flu-like symptoms did nothing to curb the illness. Patients showed signs of lung asphyxiation in the later stages and simply died from not being able to breathe any longer. Panic began to set in when the general population learned that medicine had failed them. Was this the end of humanity?

Of course, other countries were not spared. Travelers from Southwest Maine spread the disease all over the Country and overseas when they vacationed. Within a few months, the world began experiencing the frustration of being held hostage by a disease that no medical expert knew how to combat. Leadership all over the world convened to discuss options to fight the illness, as well as to stop the spread of it on a daily basis. Governments soon mandated that face masks be worn at all times. Congregation of groups of individuals were banned. Soon, stay-at-home orders were issued by local Governments in an attempt to slow the spread. Restaurants, movie theaters, gymnasiums and other business where people congregated were told to close. The economy in each Country suffered greatly as business owners were told they could not open their stores.

Many of the local retail operations closed permanently due to lack of revenue income. Soon, thousands were out of work and filing for Government Unemployment Benefits. When Government aid did not come soon enough, individuals resorted to breaking and entering. Soon, the mob began to rule despite efforts by State Governments to stop the looting and destruction of property. Law enforcement was overwhelmed. Citizens demanded answers from their elected officials who placated them with their messages of empathy. Extremist groups started to take over parts of Towns because they felt they had the answers to the problems they experienced.

Faith in government leadership vanished altogether. Anarchy reigned in the United States. And, the disease continued out of control due to the mayhem occurring world-wide. Within nine months, three million people had died from the disease all over the world. The introduction of new and effective vaccines was slow in coming with no remedy of this type in the foreseeable future.

THE FIRST ONE HUNDRED DAYS

The Town Council vote took place as scheduled with voters required to wear masks and to maintain social distancing. During the campaign, the six newcomers to the ballot aggressively canvased the Gotham populace. Their efforts paid off as each individual gained the majority vote to win his election bid. They had promised a quick resolution to the pandemic problem due to their contacts at the State level who seemed to know and promise everything.

As time wore on, grocery stores began to run out of necessary home supplies, such as, toilet paper,

paper towels, hand sanitizer and so forth. Other service organizations ran into the same problem: their main staple for sale became unavailable. Residents began seeing more and more "Going out of Business" signs as State Government mandated the closure of all indoor establishments. Gotham wasn't the only Town affected by the pandemic. Neighboring West brook, Standish and Buxton were hit even harder due to their spread out homes and clientele requiring smaller venues to shop. Local law enforcement were told to fine anyone who went into one of these smaller establishments while not wearing a mask. The news propaganda coming out of the State Capitol Augusta was that everyone had to work together to defeat this insidious disease. No one was special and everyone was susceptible. Wearing a mask and maintaining social distancing while constantly utilizing hand sanitizer were all seen as a sign of respect for one another.

Police actions against the citizens, such as fines for violating new local ordinances, were seen as

Gestapo tactics. Their ranks were viewed negatively and certain prominent citizens demanded that their actions be considered crimes against the people. The people demanded of the Town Council that funding for police protection be dramatically cut and that the money saved be used to help those who were struggling and dealing with the disease. The Council membership immediately passed such a measure with one dissenting vote. Overtime was cut and detective work was eliminated altogether. Police aggression that was required in days gone by was now seen as Police brutality and individual Officers were held accountable for their actions. Several left the Force altogether out of frustration for not being able to do their job as they were trained.

People who had lost their jobs and had no unemployment checks coming in began to band together and more than bemoan their plight. Small pockets of resistance against big business conglomerates started to take shape all over Southwest Maine. In Gotham, the businesses that were thriving were broken into and vandalized. Altercations or fights between groups occurred more and more during the late evening hours. People looked to the Town Council to do something about this dangerous activity. Their requests for assistance were not addressed or acknowledged. At the same time, the pandemic was taking life after life on a daily basis.

Individuals could not find solace in going to Church for such meetings were stopped by the local officials. No more than 10% capacity was allowed within a Church. Pastors began preaching from inside the building and broadcasting their message to those sitting in vehicles in large parking lots. Despair began to set in with not being allowed to go to work and people felt that living was no longer an option. Suicides became more common on a weekly basis. Children were not allowed to go to school and had to resort to virtual learning. Education of youth suffered greatly as a result.

There appeared to be no relief from the life that now affected the majority of the middle and lower classes. One couldn't escape to another region for everyone was experiencing the same desolation. The United States was a crumbling Republic and the rest of the world was taking note.

The Chinese appeared to be winning the battle against the disease. Their measures directed at the general populace were so strict that when a lock down occurred, everyone obeyed the standing order. Anyone who chose to resist was summarily shot. No questions were to be asked. The Chinese people were a mindless herd who reacted to every authoritarian demand. Those found to have contracted the disease were executed immediately. There were no hospitalizations for the common person. Only for the elite was the availability of medical relief. Their population masses thinned dramatically. Their military structure increased to the extent that China had the largest standing military force in the world. As the United States struggled mightily, the Chinese stood first in every living category.

As the first one hundred days came to a close, the Town of Gotham was essentially ruled by the six Council members who dictated policy without the consideration given to the people who elected them. Their actions in directing the course Gotham was to take were viewed as extreme and socialistic. Property taxes skyrocketed and individual Town taxes were applied to the purchase of any and all commodities. This was over the mandatory State tax. Cumulatively, residents had to pay 13% in tax for each item purchased no matter how small. Gotham's 7.5% Town taxation was the highest in the State of Maine. Gotham residents complained at each Council meeting but to no avail.

More and more bankruptcy filings began to inundate the Court. Finally, a blank check was essentially written to approve each request. Creditors suffered and their businesses went under. Student loans were forgiven to the delight of students, many of whom were struggling to gain a nebulous degree that wouldn't afford them a spot in the business marketplace. Universities ended up having to adjust their income bottom line.

The Governor of the State of Maine acted like a Dictator in using her power to restrict the citizens every chance she could. The pandemic was used exclusively to garner more funding from the Federal Government. This would continue as long as she declared a State of Emergency due to the Virus. The Governor was keen on wielding her power and cared very little about small businesses having to permanently close and Maine's citizens being able to attend their preferred Church services.

And all of this in the first one hundred days.

CHAOTIC DAYS

As the pandemic raged throughout the Country, Gotham citizens suffered with the despair of not having their freedom to live as they once did. Civil disobedience was the norm as it seemed as though people could not live without mayhem and destruction. Law enforcement was considered a thorn in the side of ultra left wing partisans for it interrupted the daily outline of outrage by the people who always wanted more for themselves. Racial identity was a major theme that instilled a deep hatred for anything that defied its propaganda. Coupled with lack of food, inability to find employment, living with no purpose and the prospect that nothing would ever change, Gotham residents decided not to give in without a fight.

The affluent in Town were targeted, not because they were bad people, but because they HAD. They were the big business representation that raped the economy leaving it in a terrible state. The 'economy' was fueled by the working class who were now enslaved by lack of opportunity and a reliance upon handout from the local and federal governments. They were forced to relent to the wishes of the more powerful or be denied the welfare that put food in their families' mouths.

Most of those who worked in the upper tier of industry or government were viewed as racist by position in life. If you were a corporate officer, you were against the little person who was often non-White and defenseless in a world of the powerful. Blacks and Latinos were fed the story line that they were worthless and mere pawns in the game of shameless greed. Their usefulness was non-existent, with one exception: their hatred for those who wanted to maintain the status quo, the conservative voices who were seeking to overturn the lies and deceit of big money. Those who were perceived to keep the minority population in a position of lesser status in life. Those who wanted life to return to what it always was: a middle class that served as a ceiling and prohibitive opportunity for the lower class to advance to their true worth in life. They were the cause of all of this misery and they would dearly pay for their personal injustices.

Life's scenario turned into a powder keg of disinformation that fueled everyday violence. Outside factions entered the Town and agitated those who were trying to make a living through their small businesses. If they weren't accosted verbally on the streets, their brick and mortar enterprises were vandalized.

The elderly who were considered excess to the welfare of the extreme far left of government were either dismissed as unimportant or threatened with violence if they stood up for what they perceived to be the old common core of American values. There was great danger for those over 65 years of age to walk alone in Town because the physical threat to their person would occur out of nowhere.

It was anarchy in the most evident of form.

ONE YEAR LATER IN MAINE

As promised each teen matured physically and emotionally ten years in the preceding year. They were all in the mid to upper 20s and had taken part in some political agenda or another during the past year. Each individual was endearing to those with whom he came into contact. Their attainment of State Office positions as a singular group originating from the same Town was unprecedented. Each was persuasive in his own way when in the process of 'selling' a Bill to his fellow Representative. Their ideas were cemented in socialism and their goal collectively was to eliminate the democratic way of life.

This was an election year for the Governorship in the State of Maine. Caleb had done well in terms of his political track record. He was presently the State's Senate Majority Leader and ruled his chamber personnel with authority. He was a no-nonsense Leader and was respected by all in Government. Caleb had risen to his present position when the previous Majority Leader had passed away unexpectedly. There had been friction between the Man and the Junior Senator from Gotham and a few thought that the untimely demise of the senior official may have been attributed to a rift between the two politicians. The Senior Senator had perished in an automobile accident when he was driven off the road by another motorist one evening on his way home in Scarborough. The vehicle fled the scene and, as there were no witnesses, there was no one to arrest. Caleb had been on the road that night as well and had taken the identical route to his home in Gotham.

The few politicians who knew of the disagreements between the two felt that the Junior Senator may have had something to do with the accident. It was left at that, conjecture.

Caleb canvased the State during the six-month period leading to the November election. He was definitely well received in the Cities of Poland, Augusta, Bangor, Lewiston-Auburn and Waterville as these were all ultra liberal strongholds in the State. Where he was not quite as popular was in rural Maine and Downeast where the hard-working citizens were suspicious of his socialistic views. Although he dis spend some time in these areas, he knew that acquiring votes in those sections would be difficult to attain.

His platform was a government-based agenda where the State Capitol of Augusta would dictate policy to each Town. Freedom of individual choice was ignored and very often considered contrary to the well-being of the State. Town Governments would have to adhere to the State's directives without question. His policies were right out of the books of Karl Marx and Joseph Lenin. His message was softened to the extent that he assured Mainers that their lives would be much better and more successful under his guidance and leadership. He re-assured all Mainers that his policies did not represent a dictatorial promise of lessening of individual advancement, but a hybrid selection of population-based agreement of social norms. There would be something for everyone. No one would be left behind in life. Everyone's needs would be taken care of through taxation that would be fair and equitable. For one reason or another, this argument did not seem to sit well with a certain segment of the population: the Middle Class. They would assume the majority of the tax burden.

Mainers turned out to vote in this election that promised to be a turning point in the way the State's citizens viewed the current conservative governance. It was the largest voter attendance in 30 years. When all the votes were counted and the individual Town

Halls closed, Caleb had won by a very large margin. It had been a very tight race when votes were being counted up until 6:00 pm. All of a sudden, Caleb's count dramatically increased to the point that in the end he had won 72% of the vote. The conservative candidate couldn't believe the huge margin of victory. He demanded a re-count. This was accomplished and, even though there were seeming improprieties in the vote casting, the Socialist Party claimed victory. After days of investigations into the manner in which the voting took place in every County, it was clear that fraud was involved to the extent that it favored Caleb's Party. The Conservative Party in effect 'rolled over' and conceded the election.

That evening Caleb and his five friends celebrated the victory. It was a monumental win for the socialists. Maine's liberties and freedoms were to be turned upside down now that they were under socialism. The elite were ecstatic over the win for they would become richer in the long run. The Middle Class would assume the majority of the tax burden that would have a huge impact upon their very lives. They, in effect, were going to be taking care of the Lower Class through their tax 'donations' yearly.

As the six young politicians toasted their Leader's victory, beams of light appeared suddenly in the apartment. From them materialized the Demons of Higher Authority. Their alabaster skin and dark red eyes were unnerving to several of the young men. Two of them jumped back when they first showed themselves. Caleb stood his ground and sported a calm exterior. Inwardly, he wondered what the Demons wanted this time.

As they hovered a few inches above the floor, the Leader began to speak telepathically to everyone. His message was simple: continue their work in turning the world against itself. First step: make Mainers truly understand what it means to be subservient to Government control. Secondly, work diligently to initiate a one-Party State. Undermine as much as possible the Conservative movement until their Party was in complete disarray. Thirdly, stamp out protests to their agenda by exercising force through extremist groups committed to their socialistic views. Fourth: dismantle the current law enforcement through lack of funding and the courts. Fifth: placate the citizens of Maine by showering them with Government handouts. Sixth: tax the Middle Class to the highest extent possible to break their spirit without having them admit defeat. Seventh: promote the use of emergency powers to sustain the present pandemic. Eighth: identify those who are loyal to Conservatism and create a 'Hit List' for subsequent retribution. Ninth: establish State-wide curfews to restrain the need to congregate under the guise of promoting well-being as a result of the present virus. Tenth: begin culling out of society all elderly 75 years of age and older. They were told that these were their Ten Commandments to promote the Demons Agenda. ""Do not fail us." And then, they vanished as one.

Governor Caleb and his Staff began to implement these policies on Day One. It didn't take long for Mainers to understand that Socialism as described and implemented by these Politicians was a lie and that living the community effort to produce for the State was a violation of their God-given rights. Demonstrations flared up everywhere and each was shut down quickly and effectively. Small bands of resistance began to form and these before long led to larger groups. These individuals violated those State decrees willfully and repeatedly.

THE GUBERNATORIAL TERM OF OFFICE

Caleb and his Associates adhered to the demands made by The Higher Authority to the fullest extent of their literal meaning. The tenth mandate to begin eliminating the elderly 75 years of age through attrition was met with horror and disdain. Medical treatment of this group of individuals became almost non-existent. Those who contracted the virus were refused medical attention and left to die a painful death. The main focus of attention for any and all treatment was represented in a hierarchical pyramid with Government Officials receiving first priority. From there, it was First Responders, then Big Tech Executives and so forth down to the Senior Middle Age people. Those who espoused Catholicism were excluded from receiving the new vaccine that was approved shortly after the new Governor took office.

Christian Church officials were harassed and their places of worship were soon shut down or off limits to the flock of parishioners. The Holidays of Christmas and Thanksgiving were eliminated from the calendar. Easter Sunday became just another day during the seven-day work week. Catholic priests were beaten severely if found to be conducting a Mass in secret. A number of them were even shot to death while preaching their message from the pulpit. All soon recognized that was a Government For the People whether you agreed to it or not.

In Washington, D.C., Governor Caleb had gained tremendous notoriety for his compassion shown to the poor and suffering in the State of Maine. He established shelters for many at the tax payer expense and even evicted those who had a mortgage on their homes when they could not make their monthly payments to the Bank. Within these dwellings, he let the homeless live and take over the entire property. Within the four-year term of the Governor, these neighborhoods, once beautiful, turned into slum wards. The homeless were given everything and had to work for nothing. Society was turned upside down and crime was rampant everywhere. And yet, the rich who lived behind tall electrified fences justified the actions of the poor because it was now time for equity. And these so-called philanthropists in name only became richer and richer. The Governor's popularity soared to great heights with the positive acclaim received from Washington, D.C.

Once again, six months prior to the end of the Governor's first term in Office, Caleb began setting his sights on a new goal, that of the United States Presidency. To understand how this would be possible is to realize what The Higher Authority did to manipulate the age and affairs of the six 'teens' from Gotham, Maine. During the four years in politics, each youth gained 40 years of age, 10 years for each 12 months. They were all in the 60s now and considered to be the future of the Socialist Party. Billions of dollars began flooding in to support their candidacy in the form of television ads, flights to major cities to hold rallies and effective smear campaigns against their opponents. They were the 'darlings' of the Media who fawned over them and every remark they made.

    The pandemic still raged throughout the world. Vaccines were given to those who served the needs of the Country, or State, first, followed by those in positions of necessity. The elder population began to thin out as other States adopted Maine's answer to the geriatric issue and problem of care. The 'problem' as they viewed it was that citizens 75 years of age and older were useless in terms of meeting the State's requirements. Once allowed to collect Social Security, which had been eliminated, the elderly simply were a burden on society. To care for them was to take away from the goals of the State. Time was a commodity that could not be confined, but had to be respected for its elusiveness and unyielding effects on society.

Caleb's personality and performance as Governor of the State of Maine were huge points in his favor when contrasted to his Conservative opponent. Outside influence poured into his campaign, not only from committed patrons with the United States, but also from currencies funneled through questionable resource organizations to his campaign coffers. Of course, these 'donations' had to be thoroughly 'scrubbed' for the purpose of seeming propriety for such influence peddling was entirely illegal. Receiving monetary support from foreign nationals for the purpose of gaining an elected office was considered a crime, notwithstanding alluding to an election being interfered with by a sovereign nation itself.

But these were surface issues, of course. Beneath the umbrella of propriety was a system of contributions that were received from the Chinese in the form of humanitarian grants. The receipt of these funds did not fall into the hands of their intended foundations, but rather were re-directed to Caleb's campaign effort. In a short period of time, his coffers grew to a sum never before realized by a major political candidate.

Caleb's message was clear: promote big government by having all be dependent upon its policies. Medicare for all and free college tuition were just two initiatives that represented his political platform. In terms of how to fund these and other issues, the reduction in the military budget in a huge manner would divert funds to provide for these plans. As Caleb's vision for America was to turn from present isolationism to globalization, America would be in step with the rest of the world.

The conservative Senate, notoriously weak in meeting the demands of the Democrats, had the majority for the moment. This election would identify precisely the direction the Nation was going, if the Senate majority reverted to Democratic control. With the House of Representatives already in the liberal left camp, and a Caleb victory in the White House, the Senate would need only two new members to turn the Country into an ultra liberal Nation. This was doable with the help of a secret organization that supported big government. It put its operation into high gear by focusing on the how the election process was going to play out across the Nation.

They identified six key swing States that would ultimately decide who would be in the White House. In mid-Summer, these States changed the rules for voting that enabled a mass mail-in vote without verification of the individual voter to be vetted by local government authority. A system of voter results by total count was compromised when conservative observers where deliberately excused from their assignments through intimidation by the Democratic personnel in the room. This was only one critical instance when the Constitution of the United States was fragrantly violated by the extreme left political party. During the absence of the conservative officials, millions of ballots were counted with Caleb's name as choice for President of the United States. These were forgeries and votes filled out by individuals for individuals who voted multiple times. All in all, the voting process for this General Election had been tainted with enormous fraud in favor of the Democratic Candidate, Caleb.

And when all the votes were counted, Caleb won a surprising victory in all six swing States that decided the outcome of the election. And, the Gotham Demons had everything to do with the way the election turned out through manipulation and threats of retaliation for not being an accomplice to one of the greatest fraudulent election results in American history. There would be resulting court disputes from the Right, but the results were to be of no avail in the final judgments provided.

After the inauguration of President Caleb in January, he was finally left alone in the White House to mull over the huge success of his campaign in the late evening. A spark of light appeared in the far corner of the room. It grew in intensity until a Demon appeared. Its fiery red eyes bore through those of Caleb as it floated a few feet toward the President-Elect.

Caleb began to shrink back from the specter whose noxious smell was more than nauseating. He began to vomit, but had enough control to stop it from happening. The Demon telepathically ordered him to sit down and to listen very carefully. When Caleb did so, the Demon began to tell him about a threat to his Presidency and that he needed to quell it before it took viable form.

It identified individuals who would oppose him at every turn during his first term of office. These were dangerous people who had the ability to make a difference in his establishing dominance during his political career. Caleb could not let this happen. The Demon identified them by name and where they currently lived. Caleb was ordered to take care of this threat and to do so immediately.

His initial journey to eliminate those who would oppose him would be in Gotham, Maine.

Rising Political Star

During Caleb's second month as Governor of Maine, the Town of Gotham did an entire clean sweep of the incumbents vying for re-election to the Council. Those six individuals who had mastered a negative plan to turn the welfare of the community were ousted by a large margin. In their place was one individual who had shown great promise through his campaigning for true justice and equality, not through racial identity, but through the ability of the individual to contribute to the true democratic way of life: work hard and reap the benefit of the effort given.

Timothy James O'Leary, IV was the Son of Lynn and Tim O'Leary who lived on Main Street in Gotham. The only Son of the O'Leary's was a Graduate of Clemson University and a star baseball player for the Tigers during his years in school. He was well liked by everyone and saw the good in every human being.

Tim O'Leary was an organized individual who was methodical in his approach to achieving a common sense solution to problems. He was a great listener and truly believed that everyone had an idea that could contribute positively to the organization. His intelligence level was above most and his analytical process of seeing through a problem was more than noteworthy. Tim quickly developed the trust of all of those who worked with and knew him.

He won his seat on the Council with an overwhelming majority of the vote against his opponent. When it came time to denote the Chairperson of the Council membership, all agreed that Tim was the appropriate one to stir the direction of the Town. He graciously accepted the position and promised to do what was right on behalf of the Community.

It wasn't long before his ability to lead was conspicuously noticed by State Officials in Augusta. One individual who saw the potential in Tim to rise in politics was a veteran of the Senate, Senator Ryan Brady. The latter was a true Believer in the Constitution of the United States and its implication to the fairness of all who lived in America.

Brady was a retired Naval Warrant Officer who had spent his military years as an Intelligence Analyst. He was highly decorated and even received the Navy Cross when he was temporarily assigned to Team 6 of the Navy Seals. Although he was chiefly administrative in his contribution to the boots on the ground, he had the occasion to save two of the Navy Seals during an ambush when he was temporarily assigned to the Team on a mission in Somalia. His bravery under fire marked him as an individual committed to others and to meeting the goals of the organization. When he retired, he was pushed by those who knew him well to run for political office. Seeing the disservice that was being done to the middle and lower classes, he reluctantly agreed to attempt to make a difference to those in need. The people responded by electing him to a Senate seat in the Maine Legislature.

As O'Leary took the reigns of the Town Council and began to improve the welfare of the people of Gotham through a common sense approach to business, his notoriety grew throughout the State. Others in neighboring communities began to seek his advice and to ask him how his new policies for the Town were enhancing attitudes toward community involvement. He responded by saying that to have empathy and to react upon it in ways that were accessible was to see the results being fulfilled for the benefit of the intended. His model of governing was an example of an individual being for the people and not the other way around. Sometimes, his decisions were difficult, but, in the end, they were always for the welfare of the most in need.

One evening when he was in the Council chambers alone doing some strategic planning, he heard a strange buzzing sound coming from outside the room and in the hallway. Before he could get to the door to see what was going on, a bright light appeared in front of him not more than five feet away. Tim stood still and watched it materialize into a human form.

What stood before him was a being that was grotesque in features. It had piercing red eyes and its skin complexion was alabaster white. It said and did nothing until Tim heard in his mind that he was to sit down immediately. When O'Leary balked, he was pushed violently toward a chair in the middle of the room, not by a physical shove, but by a mind controlled physical contact.

He was nearly upended but caught himself as he slammed against the backing of the seat. The Demon floated to within three feet of him and stopped. He began to 'talk' to Tim telepathically.

"You have meddled in the affairs of this Town too soon and too much. You will cease your attempt to correct what has been given to you prior to the election. As the citizens are approving of your methods in governing, they will have no problem when you change your position to reflect a socialistic viewpoint. In other words, you will continue the policies of the previous Council, or you will pay for your disobedience with your life and soul. This is your one and only warning. There will be no communicating between us should we have to meet again."

At that moment, a huge wolf-like creature came charging through the doorway and rushed the Demon. It leaped at it and before it could make contact, the specter had vanished. It sniffed about and went to the door and looked out into the corridor. It turned around and came over to Tim where it sat down. Its blue eyes were brilliant. It did nothing at first and then it morphed into a human being, a man approximately six feet two inches with a well toned body. It pulled up another chair beside O'Leary and sat down. Before saying anything for a few seconds, it studied Tim.

"In our world, Timothy O'Leary, you are well respected for your convictions and steadfast belief in the goodness of man. My name is Resdin and I have been asked to keep you safe by The Entity. Wherever you go, I will not be far behind. You may encounter that Demon again, but I promise you that no harm will befall you."

Resdin got up slowly and walked to the doorway. Before leaving the room, he turned and encouraged O'Leary to continue on his path of doing what was right and decent for the people of Gotham. There were those who were watching him and protecting him from all evil. Then he was gone.

Tim continued to sit in the chair and tried to fathom what had just happened. For some reason, he was not frightened by the event, but actually felt more emboldened to continue his present course of action for the people of Gotham. Tim was familiar with the concept of The Entity for his Father had come in contact with this Intergalactic Being in the past. The stories about how his Dad and his Friend Hunter vanquished the shape shifters and Indian who rose from the dead were not lost on him. Sir Shawn Crawford had played a major role in protecting the Town, as did their Primary Care Physician, Dr. Marty Wesolowski. It was a story well worth writing, Tim thought. And, it looked like another was in the process with these unexpected visits from both the Demon and Wolf.

He left the Town Hall and drove home. When he arrived, he found Sir Shawn Crawford, Christopher, Hunter and Colette waiting for him in front of the house. Tim got out of his vehicle and walked over to the group.

"Sir Shawn and Hunter, what a very pleasant surprise! And Christopher and Colette as well. What brings you all to my humble home? Please come inside."

O'Leary offered them a drink while they got settled in the two bedroom apartment. They graciously said no and apologized for showing up at this hour. Tim said that no apology was necessary. It was always good to see Friends from the future anytime.

"What can I do for you?" Tim asked.

"Timmy, your life is in danger. Of course, you already know that from the visit you had with the Demon in your office this evening. Yes, we know all about it," said Shawn.

"It's a good thing that Resdin was nearby to stop the Demon from causing you any harm," added Christopher. Hunter concurred.

"Word gets around pretty quickly around Gotham, but impromptu meetings with evil beings at night, how did you know?" asked Tim.

"The Entity asked us to keep tabs on you, Tim. He needs you to stay safe during these tough political times. The Country is a powder keg at the moment given the socialistic actions by the far left Democratic Party. And, with the new President-Elect, the situation is only going to worsen. There are those who believe that this is your time to come forward and steer this Country in another direction.

"You know as well as I do that people are suffering and that the new regime in Washington wants everyone under their control. Dissent is not an option under the pending leadership. The Entity sees what is going on and a remedy is needed to 'right the ship', so to speak," said Crawford.

There was a knock on the door. Tim got up from his chair and went over to open it. Standing on the door step was a young girl of about 12 years of age. She smiled at him and walked into the apartment without saying a word. Shawn and Christopher saw her and both broke out in a huge smile.

"Emily!" exclaimed Colette. "What are you doing here? And, how did you get here from 2078 Australia?"

"It's really a short story. I am here to reinforce the safety net for Tim who, by the way, may need the power of the Amulet in his battle against the Demons."

She pulled out the ancient Amulet from around her neck and showed it to all. It gleamed in the overhead light. Tim stepped aside and let her in. She patted Tim on the shoulder as she stepped by and went over to the couch to sit. Shawn marveled at her grace as she passed by him.

Emily was an Agent of The Entity. She had been another who was instrumental in defeating the demons in Gotham many years ago. Hanging from her neck was an Amulet that had the power to destroy evil. It dated back to the Third Crusades circa 1197 A.D.

She was a 'perpetual teen' in that she never aged. Her 12 years of age appearance deceived many who thought her to be a frail young girl incapable of defending herself. Many a mound of demon ash would prove that notion to be wrong.

There was a scratching at the door and Tim got up to see what that was all about. When he opened it, Resdin was sitting there calmly, in wolf-like form. He got up and trotted into the room and sat down by Emily and Colette.

"Hello, Resdin, somehow I knew I would see you again. How is your King doing back in the 12th Century?" Emily asked.

If you've never seen a wolf talk, and you probably haven't, this was an experience to savor. Resdin responded by saying that His Highness was doing well, but complaining always about the smallest of ailments. Above that, he was tirelessly involved in a civil war somewhere which ran himself and the other Knight-Wolves ragged.

"The King got himself involved in a cabbage patch dispute that led to farmers and their wives pulling out pitch forks to defend their land against a Duke who mistakenly thought the land was his. Imagine that, a cabbage patch and women throwing pitch forks. If it had happened, it would have been a sight to see, I tell you."

Christopher chuckled and told him that it was good to see him once again. "How is that wound doing? Has it bothered you over these many years, Resdin?"

"No, Christopher, thanks to you and your life-saving measure, I have had no problem with it at all. It was lucky for me that you were with Sir Shawn that day in our battle with the Saracens."

"I'm glad to hear that you're doing well, Resdin. What brings you to Tim's apartment so soon after your confrontation with the Demon this evening?"

The wolf turned toward Tim and told him that there was a solid rumor that the new President-Elect had taken note of his political progress and that there was concern about Tim's growing popularity with the people. There was even mentioned that friends of the President-Elect were being sent to Gotham to monitor your every move on and off the Town Council.

"These are not nice people, Tim. If they feel that you are a conservative threat to their agenda, they will stop at nothing to eliminate you immediately. Case in point: a Representative attempted to counter act a policy initiative by then Governor Caleb that would have taxed the people of Maine unfairly. The day before the vote was taken, the man was killed in an 'accident' on the highway leading to his home. There was one witness who thought that he had been forced off the road when a heavy duty pickup truck swerved toward him suddenly causing the politician to lose control of his car. The man went down an embankment and hit a tree going at least 60 miles an hour.

"The next day, the vote was canceled altogether because many feared that this act was retaliation against the conservatives not supporting the Governor's tax proposal. No one could prove that the accident was an intentional act to sabotage a political agenda promoted by the Governor."

There was a banging on the roof of the one-story apartment. It sounded like someone had jumped or landed on it. Simultaneously, two bright lights showed through the windows from the front lawn. Resdin yelled, "Get down!!"

An arc of light smashed through two windows and struck the far wall in the living room. One quarter of the wall was disintegrated. Resdin was quickly on the move and jumped out one of the windows breaking glass on the edges as he leaped to the ground. Shawn and Christopher ran out the door to the outside and peered upward toward the roof. Hunter went around to the back through the kitchen door. A demonic being was using its arc light powers to burn a hole through the shingles.

Christopher stood very still and focused on the Demon above. His entire body turned into a bluish covering. His eyes shot forward a blue thin laser line of energy that struck the Demon in the chest and causing the being to topple over backwards.

Meanwhile, Resdin had knocked one of the two Demons down on the lawn and had it by the neck. The other was about to strike the wolf with its arc light when Emily appeared in the doorway and pointed her amulet in its direction. A thick spark of fire shot forth and hit the Demon in the chest. Its body exploded inwardly and pieces of body tissue was strewn about the lawn and nearby sidewalk.

Resdin completed his aggressive task by ripping out the throat of the Demon. The wolf got up and howled over the being's lifeless eyes. It then turned around and faced the others before sitting down on the grass. Resdin looked to the roof and saw what was left of Christopher's work and nodded to the boy. He got up and walked slowly over to Emily and said, "I owe you my life, Little Girl. I will forever be in your debt." Hunter came around the corner of the home from the backyard at that moment.

"What did I miss, Coach?"asked King.

They moved the only body of the three that was left relatively whole over and behind a string of low lying bushes on the side of the home. They had just put it on the ground when Gotham Rescue showed up with lights and sirens going. They checked with Tim about any injuries that may have occurred. He assured the medical personnel that all were fine and thanked them for their service.

The Fire Department arrived two minutes later and prepared to extinguish any fires that were still burning. The Chief came over to Shawn and Tim and remarked about the lightning show that just occurred over the Town. He told Tim that he was sorry that his home was the only one hit. The Unit carried out its investigation of the property and left.

As the fire trucks drove away, Christopher knelt over what was left of Resdin's victim. He noted that the synapses in the head were still sparking and that this being could still be alive. The boy turned toward Shawn who was now greeting the arrival of Tim's parents. He looked back at the form lying there and made a decision to explore through telepathy the thoughts that went through the Demon's mind within the previous six hours. That was all the time he thought he could extract information from the being.

Tim came over to Shawn and said that he was staying at his parents house for the time being and that if they didn't have a place to stay, they were welcome to come along as well. Crawford replied that they already had made plans. Emily voiced the same regards and thanked Tim for his generosity. The O'Leary's then left for their home on Main Street.

As they were driving away, Christopher walked back to the bushes and knelt down beside the

Demon's body. Shawn, Resdin and Emily joined him and asked what he was doing. The boy said that he was running a diagnostic of the brain waves of the being to try to ascertain a motive for the attack this evening.

Christopher placed a hand on either side of the Demon's head and closed his eyes. Once again, a bluish tint covered the boy from head to foot until one could barely see him within the nebulous shroud. Christopher remained in this state for a good five minutes before the tinted covering began to dissipate.

When he opened his eyes, he immediately sat down and drew in some deep breaths. He remained silent for another moment and then looked at the others before him. He stood up and nearly collapsed, but Shawn caught him. Resdin had materialized into his human shape and he helped Shawn bring Christopher into Tim's home. They sat the boy down and gave him some water to drink. Christopher then began to relate to the others what he had seen.

The Demons goal was to bring down humanity through socialistic annihilism. They were forcing people to turn on others so as to deny them individualistic freedom and liberty. The end game was to have one individual left at the top who controlled everyone akin to an ancient Emperor or Czar. The identity of such an individual was not to be known in the future, but he was already prepared to assume the role of National Ruler. His name was President-Elect Caleb.

The Demons were sent to Tim's home because they saw him as a threat to their achieving their objectives. O'Leary's popularity was soaring as he was already being noticed in other States for his conviction to do what was right, his amazing ability to bring people together and his organizational skills that made sense to the common person.

Tim was absolutely committed to personal freedom and the right for the individual to control his own destiny in life. Individualistic motivation to succeed was important to fuel the fires of innovation and new ideas. Everyone has an idea, some better than others, but have all be aired for examination. The fundamental block that built such a society was the belief in the individual and his ability to succeed, and fail, but to try again. The human spirit was strong and imaginative. It fed off the desire to compete not only with others, but with himself to improve upon what he had become. Life was not static, but was all about changes and the ability to adapt. Successful civilizations showed that individuals who were able to agree to disagree were promoting a wealth of ideas leading to suppositions and eventual laws of nature, science and those developed as a result of entrepreneurship.

SOARING POLITICAL ADVANCES

The three Demons who were eliminated by Shawn and the others had represented a Council member each when they first arrived. When their lives were spared, they were assured of continued living as long as the Demon that represented him was alive. When the beings were killed, each individual past Council member immediately succumbed to a massive heart attack at the very same moment in their homes. Their souls were carried back to the clearing where they first encountered the Demons. As their spirits approached the open area, a small fire erupted in the middle of the circular ground. The souls fell quickly into the flames. Shrieks of pain could be heard for brief seconds and then silence. A moment later, the flames extinguished themselves leaving no burnt mark in the earth.

Tim O'Leary's tenure as Chairman of the Town's Council was a complete success. He mandated that Town businesses remain open so as to promote the economic well-being. His openness about ignoring the so-called scientists warnings about increased deaths due to the virus was appreciated by all. Gotham's Town's people appeared to be the only segment of the State's population that carried on its daily life without regard for the pandemic. Other County citizens took note and forced their Town Selectmen to follow Gotham's example. Before long, the State of Maine was the only State in the Country who normalized its daily living for its citizens.

Neighboring States took note and its people forced their community Governments to eliminate the 'shackles' of confinement affecting the economic prosperity of small businesses everywhere. New England States all followed suit as Maine led the way in disputing the so-called experts dire predictions that the people would eventually pay for their 'misguidance'.

Two years into O'Leary's leadership on the Gotham Council, half the Country was ignoring the professional medical authority that insisted people stay home, self-isolate and disallow large gatherings. Those that adhered to these warnings in the remaining States were affected by large numbers of suicides and despair. The State Governors utilized the police to enforce large gatherings, more than five in a home, from convening even during Thanksgiving and Christmas. By the time New Year's had come and gone, the people confined in these few States had had enough and began demonstrating in mass numbers. Their voices were heard through elections as left-wing socialist leadership failed in its attempt to continue its radical stewardship of its people. By the end of Tim's third year as Council Chair in

Gotham, 95% of the States had followed his example of liberating its citizens from the bondage of the virus. It was no wonder that he began getting pressure from all segments of the population to run in the next Presidential election occurring the following November.

During the three years that Tim O'Leary had defied the virus from taking control of people's lives, President Caleb's popularity had sunk below a 25% approval rating. His chances of being re-elected on his socialistic platform agenda appeared bleak. His staff had seen what was going on initially in Gotham and a few had begun to warn him that the Town's stance on ignoring the virus was becoming more and more popular, When O'Leary declared that he would run for President that November, Caleb received a visit from the three remaining Demons.

One evening while he was mulling over his political future in the White House, he saw three beams of light appear in the outside corridor. Their intensity was not the customary gentle appearance, but rather hard and rough looking. The Demons had just arrived and they were not pleased with Caleb. His lack of response to what was happening across the Country in terms of losing control of State Governments was unacceptable. It was time for a wake up call to the President of the United States and the beings were not so gentle about providing their message of disappointment to the Chief Executive.

Shawn Crawford and the others had remained away from Gotham, Maine during the three years of Tim's term of Office on the Town Council. Resdin had been steadfast in his protection of O'Leary through the years, even though the threat of Demon retaliation never materialized.

AS the Spring months turned to Summer, donations to Tim's campaign began pouring in by the thousands of dollars. In July, he selected Resdin, the Human, to be his running mate. Tim not only had a personal shape shifting Bodyguard, but had a solid connection to The Entity and to the Crawford Family, if assistance was needed. He was assigned a Secret Service Detail in addition.

His campaign platform was based on individualism and the freedom to choose. Tim's message was clear: respect the rights for all. Time and time again, his rallies were well received and the support he received was enormous.

Conversely, Caleb struggled in his attempt to foster the ideas of his first term in Office. People were turned off by his rhetoric. It was as if the Nation was now free as it embraced his opponent's attitude toward returning to the normalization of life as it once was prior to the pandemic, Caleb couldn't compete with this and his status with the people who had supported him initially dwindled to a hard core group of fanatics who decided to take matters into their own hands.

DEMONIC RETALIATION

The Demons were outraged with the lack of acceptance of Caleb's political views by the people and decided to intervene directly by promoting left wing riots in the streets across the Nation. These were met with law enforcement support resulting in a quick and speedy stop to these occurrences of mayhem. More direct measures began to take place against Tim's safety in the weeks leading up to the November Election.

One afternoon when traveling by ground transportation to a major political rally in a southern city, his small convoy was stopped by train traffic at one of the many rail crossings threading their way across the State. As he sat in the back seat and pouring over his speech he was to deliver, hundreds of beams of light appeared on the horizon at high altitude. They appeared to advance slowly toward Tim's small group of vehicles and descending at the same time.

The atmosphere quickly changed from a clear day to one of ominous skies. Huge black clouds billowed out of nowhere above the beams of light now looking like strings of electricity hanging menacingly over the land. The electricity in the air was noticed by all as it grew in intensity. The strings of light thickened and grew brighter the closer they got to the ground, now directly in front of the stationary vehicles.

As the tips of these electrical discharges from the clouds reached ground level, a clap of thunder sounded and shook the ground. The beams now numbered in the hundreds and hung like a white electrified curtain before Tim's small group of vehicles.

The clouds continued to thicken and the day turned nearly into night. From the electrical discharges, individual forms began to take shape very slowly. The light intensity emanating from these forms grew to nearly a blinding wall of white. Then it began to lessen very slowly until what stood before the convoy were hundreds of demon-like creatures. They slowly advanced toward Tim's vehicles in a methodical manner. The atmosphere grew darker and the only light was from the advancing beings.

Suddenly, an extremely loud clap of thunder was heard and an intense blue light appeared in the sky overhead. It swirled about swiftly and formed a cloud mass that grew in intensity. As it spread outward, an eye in the center opened very slowly. Its circumference continued to expand until the small aperture became enormous.

Several loud earth shaking thunderous sounds were heard one after the other, each greater in intensity. Out of the huge opening in the center of the blue cloud formation came aircraft by the dozens.

These were futuristic aerial platforms never before seen by man. One by one they descended toward what looked like a tremendous hoard of Demons advancing on O'Leary's vehicles.

Just as the beings reached the lead vehicle in the small group, an aircraft fired laser after laser striking down each form with a resounding thunderous sound. Other fighters followed the first and began firing their weapons at the sea of Demons below them. The human-like forms were pummeled by laser hits time and time again by the aircraft flying their individual diving runs on the demonic masses.

This activity continued for more than 15 minutes before all of the beings were neutralized on the ground. Aircraft continued to circle the group of vehicles until they climbed quickly into the center of the bluish cloud and disappeared from view. All but one, however.

The futuristic fighter hover landed some 50 feet from Tim's vehicle and the pilot spooled down the engines. When the turbines stopped turning, a ladder dropped from the belly of the aircraft and the pilot stepped down to the ground. As he walked toward Tim who was standing with the others by their vehicles, he took off his helmet and waved.

"Shawn, I should have known that it was you leading the cavalry from the skies! We on the ground thought it was all over when those Demons descended upon us. Thank goodness that you were nearby!" exclaimed Tim.

"Well, we weren't exactly nearby by accident, Tim. We had forewarning of the attack on your group of vehicles 20 minutes prior to it starting. It appears that The Entity never lost track of what the Demons were up to and alerted me and the others you saw to come to your assistance through the Dimensional Gateway. My whole Family got involved with flying those fighters. I think Colette had the most fun followed by Nate Doerfler and Bob Gonzales.

"I'll be watching more closely your every move during your campaign in the few remaining days before the Election. Everyone from 2078 sends his and her best wishes to you, Tim, as you continue to travel and campaign these last few weeks. Good luck the rest of the way, Tim."

One would have thought that the interference into O'Leary's quest for the Presidency was no longer a factor. There were three remaining Demons who had not been accounted for during the attack. These three were of the original six to arrive initially in Gotham. The Leader took the other two into seclusion temporarily as a final measure to effect an attack plan the conservative politicians would never see coming.

Tim continued his campaigning up to the day before the major Election in November. His approval rating reached 85% as the day drew near for the Country's citizens to vote. President Caleb's campaign was in a dismal state as he garnered less and less attention when he gave his speeches on socialism and the 'benefits' thereof.

A hard core contingent of ultra left wing fanatics continued to pop up wherever Tim traveled. They attempted to disrupt the momentum by harassing those loyal to the conservative movement. Their efforts were futile as the masses fought back against such violence. Seeing that this left wing tactic was not working, big business leadership pumped more money to agitate into the final weeks.

Tim's life was threatened repeatedly via mail and through social media. The Press, or Media General, portrayed O'Leary as someone without qualifications and spun lies about his character, They even fabricated false stories about his past and bombarded the airwaves with conjecture that served to sow the seeds of doubt about him to the public at large. There was absolutely nothing they wouldn't do to sway the voters away from this political darling.

The Secret Service worked around the clock to investigate threats against Tim. His detail remained small in concert with the provisions of safety for those vying for high public office. They couldn't be everywhere and took chances with leaving certain areas left unchecked during campaign stops.

DAYS OF DANGER

On the morning of the Election, Tim set out to vote with his Secret Service Detail in tow. He arrived in a Lincoln SUV at the polling place that was packed with voters. A line to get into the building extended two blocks away from the entrance.

As he exited the vehicle, a man dressed in a business suit pulled out a small .380 pistol and fired it directly at O'Leary. The round entered his torso below the heart and he collapsed to the pavement. Secret Service immediately shot the gunman and he went down beside Tim.

One of the Agents applied pressure to Tim's wound as O'Leary began to go into shock and then lost consciousness. An ambulance arrived on the scene three minutes later and technicians immediately began working on O'Leary. After being loaded within the emergency vehicle, it roared off to the nearest Trauma Center arriving there within 10 minutes. By this time, Tim O'Leary was non-responsive. He was pronounced dead in the operating room five minutes later.

Tim saw his body lying on the gurney inside the ambulance as he floated above it. He felt no pain and wondered what had happened. The memory of being shot point blank came to him, as well as seeing his shooter going down to the pavement after he was shot. For a brief moment, O'Leary wondered about his assailant and hoped that he was alright.

He sat down in the spacious back area of the vehicle and looked to his left. Sitting beside him were Christopher and Colette Crawford. They both smiled at him and Colette patted him on his knee.

"Tim," she began, "You are going to pull through this fine. You will be pronounced dead upon arrival at the Hospital, but in reality, your vital signs are being masked temporarily. This day belongs to you, Tim, and you are going to be alive to see it through to the end. Christopher and I will see that you are taken care of and that your return to life will be a positive sign to people that your work here on Earth is not completed. The man who shot you, in effect, sealed your Presidency."

At that moment, Tim found himself in a room filled with people that he recognized. Coming over to greet him was Shawn and his Wife Christine.

"Timmy, congratulations on your winning the Presidency. You will be one of the very best the Country will ever have. The Entity has taken the liberty of having you sequestered just for a short time so that those around you here may wish you good fortune and share some insight into what you may expect as President of the United States. Here is one Gentleman who I know will be enlightening."

A tall bearded man sauntered forth with a hand extended and said, "Mr. President, it is my honor to meet such a Conservative who loves the people as much as he does his Country. I know you will do great things in the years ahead. Never deter from your beliefs, Timothy, for those were the principles that got you to the very top. Best of luck to you, young man."

Abraham Lincoln then walked over to the side to allow the next two individuals to approach. The first extended his hand as he smiled broadly and said in a strong New England accent, "Well, my boy, you certainly know how to make an entry into the White House. My Brother, Robert here, and I know that you will excel in your work to serve the needs of all people in the United States in the years ahead. Congratulations on your victory and we wish you well, President O'Leary."

John and Bobby Kennedy then stood aside. A heavy set man came forward and didn't extend his hand in congratulations, but wrapped Tim up in his arms and kissed him on the cheek. Dr. Martin Luther King, Jr. held O'Leary at arms length and smiled broadly.

"You know, Mr. President, I had a dream one day and you were actually in it. As a matter of fact, you played an important part in healing the wounds the Country suffered during the past few years. I wish I were alive today to work with you side by side to see the vision of people working and living together in harmony. This is going to be a momentous time for you, my Son. And, you are the only one to insure that, because of your leadership, the Country and the world will be a safer place to be. Congratulations, Mr. President."

Bob Gonzales and Nathan Doerfler stood close by and wished him well, as did Tim and Grace O'Hara, Michael and Allison Morrison, Admiral J. Hunter King, Emily and Resdin. He stood before them all feeling very humbled by their presence. As he waved his appreciation to everyone, the crowd broke out in a thunderous cheer of good will.

Resdin walked over and said, "Well, Mr. President, I do believe it's time to return so that all will see that you are fine and ready to begin your duties as the Chief Executive of the United States. And, Sir, I am honored to serve with you as your Vice-President. Shall we go, Mr. President?"

A soft blue thin cloud of air appeared and wrapped itself around Tim O'Leary until no one in the room was visible. He opened his eyes in a spacious room with numerous bright lights shining around him. He blinked twice and stared up at an individual dressed in scrubs. The Doctor, Tim presumed, dropped whatever he had in his hands and his eyes went wide in disbelief. "He's back!!"

Several people began to scurry all about him. The Surgeon standing above him said, "Sir, I really thought we had lost you! I have no idea what just happened, but I do believe I have witnessed a modern day miracle!"

He then turned his attention to those around him and began giving orders. Another Doctor who had been assisting him was told to go out to the waiting room and announce that Tim O'Leary had survived and was resting comfortably. A few minutes later, a roar of approval could be heard out in the waiting area. Many questions followed about why he had been pronounced dead in the first place. No logical answer could be given.

FINAL VOTE AND JUSTICE

President Timothy James O'Leary, IV was sworn in as the 47th President of the United States on that cold January 20th morning in Washington, D.C. He felt no ill effects from the shooting two months prior and was prepared to execute the duties set before him by the people of the Country. Tim's Parents stood close by and watched the ceremony with pride. Vice-President Resdin was to be sworn in aside from this ceremony that did not have President Caleb in attendance. The latter had contracted the virus that had roared through the Country and he was considered to be deathly ill.

Back in Gotham, Maine, Nathan Doerfler and Tim O'Hara had arrived from 2078 and through the Dimensional Gateway to take care of some last minute business for the President.

They were in the Gotham Cemetery and proceeded to three sets of tomb stones that were lying side by side. Nathan took out two vials containing a white powdery substance. He gave one to O'Hara and they proceeded to spread the contents over three graves. When the substance hit the ground, it immediately infused itself into the earth. They both waited for 30 seconds and then heard a loud wailing coming from beneath the ground.

The graves they had chosen were the temporary resting places of the only three Demons remaining from the original six. The powder was a deadly poison that corrupted the soil so that nothing could survive in it or on it. The two men walked calmly away.

At that moment, three former Gotham Council Members succumbed to massive heart attacks simultaneously.

The Demons of Gotham, Maine were no more.

AUTHOR BIBLIOGRAPHY

TIMOTHY JAMES LTC O'LEARY, III is a retired U.S. Army Lieutenant Colonel with 27 years of active duty and reserve service to his Country. Tim served a tour of duty in both Vietnam and the First Persian Gulf Wars. He is a graduate of the Defense Language Institute in Monterey, California where he earned a diploma in Italian Language training. Tim is a helicopter pilot with 2,200 hours of flight time in UH-1 and

OH-58 aircraft with the United States Army. During Operation Desert Storm, Tim was a medevac pilot with the 217th Medical Battalion. His final tour of duty was Battalion Commander of the 286th Supply and Service Battalion.

He has a B.A. degree in Sociology and French, and holds a Master of Education and Educational Specialist degrees in Educational Administration and Supervision from Georgia Southern College. Tim was a Doctor of Education degree candidate at the University of Virginia in Educational Administration and Supervision. He also has one year of Spanish Language training at the University of Southern Maine in Poland. Tim taught foreign language and social studies in the Georgia public school system for three years and was an assistant principal at a secondary education school in Virginia.

Tim has run 13 marathons to include the Marine Corps in 1994 and Boston's 100th in 1996. He has been a baseball umpire for over 40 years and has officiated five Cal Ripken World Series. Tim has umpired two Eastern Regional Softball Tournaments in Connecticut and was chosen to umpire the Africa/Europe Regional Softball Tournament in The Netherlands in July 2021.

He played Varsity Baseball at Georgia Southern and was a Player for the European All-Star Continental Cavaliers that toured South Africa in 1972.

Tim has three children and five grandchildren. He and his Wife Lynn reside in Gorham, Maine.

www.ingramcontent.com/pod-product-compliance
Lightning Source LLC
LaVergne TN
LVHW041609070526
838199LV00052B/3055